you dese

First paperback edition July 2021

Designed by Aaliyah Vines

ISBN: 978-1-0879-6541-3

To my father, for always supporting my dreams.
To my mother, for always wiping away the tears.
To both of you, for giving me wings.
And letting me fly free.

. . .

So much of my book is about friendship, because you need
people who can help you grow.
Who can help you see the world a little bit clearer.
Who can help you put down the pencil long enough to live.
Serenity, Ella, Mallory. This is to you.
To friendship. To never forgetting to live.

table of contents

I didn't know
where to go
what to do
who to be
and just as I began
to feel completely
hopelessly lost
the moon whispered to me
write
so I did
I emptied myself
onto the pages
I bled dry
through my pen
and found myself
sitting there
right in front of me

the dark

enjoy the journey
as much as the destination.
"I am" I say
as every day I run myself ragged
and every night I cry
because I'm not good enough

-burnout-

I can never slow
or rest
I've been running
so long
and so fast
trying to keep up
with the standards
I raised for myself
but what about when I trip?
I'll never catch up
to where I was
so I keep running
until my feet bleed

my body is bound together
by stories left untold
and thoughts that go on forever
and I try and act bold
but my words stumble
and fall to the ground
and I hear them all mumble
like they didn't hear a sound
so I try it again
and the second's just like the first
and I try and think of when
did my lips become so cursed?

I used to apologize
for existing
I went without
so that I would not be a bother
I shrank
so I wouldn't get in everyone's way
and now I find it
so hard not to be ignored
everyone got used to me being a shadow
and now they walk right through me

every second of my life
is spent with me, myself, and I
yet I tried for everyone's approval
but mine

I can blame no one but myself
for thinking I was broken and never asking for
help
I can't explain why I felt that way
just that I was never okay at the end of the day

in the end we're all just stories
I hope it's a happy story
but the good ones never are

I woke up
even though I had hoped
that I wouldn't
so now I prayed
that if I had to wake up again
it would at least be
as someone different

I dig
my own grave
but it's so addictive
I don't think
I'll ever stop
I drink self hatred
like whiskey

-and do shots at 1am-

I pushed and pulled and crunched
until my pants hung from my hips
and the number on the scale was double digits
and my bones shown through my skin
but the face I saw in the mirror
looked the same
and the insults in my head
never changed

I don't know why
it's so hard to love myself
why is it predetermined
that I will hate my body
and my skin
and my hair
why is my mind
so against me

waiting
for the end
of the day
the words
I'm okay
on replay
they sound
rehearsed
even to me

-I'm okay-

at least you're here
at least you survived
yes but it's been far too long
since I actually felt alive

do I even deserve
the right to the word
depression
when it's all really
in my own head
when all of my problems
come from my own mind
and my own bad decisions

-even my depression has imposter syndrome-

you don't look sick
oh sweetie
I'm dying inside

how do you explain to someone
that you don't have the energy
to be around other people
that you don't even have the energy
to be around yourself

it only took so many times
of hearing
your life is so perfect
what do you have to complain about?
before I stopped asking for help
and started blaming myself

it doesn't always follow
the end of the world
sometimes
on a Saturday
or a Tuesday
I'll just be in the shower
or reading in my bed
or maybe out with friends
and it will hit me
again
and again
until I'm just staring
into space
thinking
sinking
drowning
I spiral inwards
and it never ends

-because depression doesn't care if you're doing better-

in spite
of how hard I've tried
I still have nights
where the only thing I do is ache

the only therapy I could afford
was at 4am
on Monday nights
I paid in tears
so that I could hear
it's all your fault
on repeat

too many voices
too many sights
too much going on
too many lights
I try and focus
breathe it all out
I try and figure out
what this is all about
my vision is blurry
and I can't see
and I just think
please don't talk to me
I feel like I've lost
control over my thoughts
as they rush by so fast
they can't be caught
my hands are sweaty
and my throat is tight
and I know I've got
to be quite a sight
they all know I won't make it

to the end of the year
look she's trying
to hold back tears
they ask
if I'm okay
I smile and say
"It's just been a long day"

on and on
thoughts fly by
they keep me up
late at night
I choke on them
hard to breathe
sends me falling
to my knees
million thoughts
spiraling down
no end in sight
none to be found
wait it out
now it's dawn
thoughts still fly
on and on

-thought spiral-

there are days where I don't know what light is
and days where it's all I see
there are days where there's a thousand voices
and days where it's just me
sometimes there's a drought
not a drop in sight
and sometimes there's a flood
and I sink to the bottom where its dark as night
some days I want to explore the world
and sometimes I just want to go home
some days I feel like I'm deserted
and some days I'm never alone
but whether light or dark
I'm always falling apart

she sounded mad
what did I do?
was I rude?
or selfish again?
did I say something stuck up?
you have a knack for that
and for losing friends
yes they all get tired of me eventually
because you're boring and rude
and lifeless and a bit of a prude
they wish you weren't here
maybe even dead-
enough
I think I ought to go to bed

in the end
I couldn't blame anyone
for how I felt
it was in my DNA

-chemical imbalance-

for too many years
my only true friends
the ones who never left
were Harry Potter
the Moon
and my Insecurities

thank you for making me feel like it was okay to exist

-a girl who loved the rain before the hurricane came-

your waves are tearing
at my shore
I don't know if I can take it
anymore
but I stay around
I don't know what for
and wait for something
anything
an open door

I let you in
knowing the consequences
knowing how it felt
to be left
I handed you the knife
and told you to hold me

I'm getting to where I think about you less and less
but you're still the only thing I can write about

there are songs
and poems
and novels
written on broken hearts
caused by broken lovers
but where's my song
about best friends
that became strangers
and best friends
that became bullies
and best friends
that will always be what ifs
where's my sonnet?
don't make me sit with my mistakes
in silence
it's too close to insanity

in the aftermath of you I had to glue myself back together…

… I'm still not sure everything's in the right place

I lay in bed
staring at the ceiling
going over the words you threw
I would have been
able to dismiss them
if I knew any self worth
but I didn't
so
I lay in bed
staring at the ceiling
going over the words you threw
until they were in my blood
in my brain
until they were true

we tear
each other down
trying to build
ourselves up
and both end up in ruin

you test me to see if I break
and then don't listen when I tell you I'm broken

never doubt the power your words have over people
they are a weapon best left unwielded
I should know
I have gotten and given many scars from said weapon

why'd you have to look at me
like my very existence
was tiresome

you play victim
while your knife
is still in my back
and my blood
is still fresh on your lips

you're out there
somewhere
God knows where
with a collection of secrets I told you
while I was half drunk on sleep
and all I'm left with
is a wound almost too deep
the fact that you never loved me

maybe you'll miss me
maybe you won't
I kind of hope you do
I kind of hope you don't

a shadow of my past now
an echo of sound
but still I really hope
I won't see you around

I tossed all the pictures
and deleted all the texts
I'm forgetting about you
and moving on to what's next

I'm in a better place now
and it's easier to see
that you weren't my prince charming
just another lesson for me

I lost myself
in the idea of you
waiting for the fantasy
to finally come true

isn't this such a familiar song?
same lyrics different beat
but I hit play anyway
and put you on repeat

-"*I would never hurt you*"-

it was so hard
to get over you
because there was no end
you left midsentence
leaving me to wait
for you to come back
and finish our story

slowly I began to realize
that you are not who I thought
and I still come back
again and again
because our fragile fairy tale
was better than the ugly reality

I loved and I lost
but what I lost wasn't you
I lost myself in the lies
when the truth was due

I don't really wish
I were dead
I just wish
that I could start living
completely
fully
without fear

we sit in front of these glowing screens
for hours
while outside sits the world
waiting to be explored
we watch snaps and reels and stories
until the sun sets
and then we sleep and do it all again
and I am left with this longing
for adventure
for air
for freedom
I a left with the voices in my head
chanting *carpe diem*
I am left with the desire to seize life by the throat
and never let go
I want new and exciting
I want memories
I want Friday nights
that could lead us to the end of the earth
and back
but I still sit here

scrolling
waiting
for something to happen
like it's a modern day plague
with no cure

my worst fear
the thing that haunts my dreams at night
is living the rest of my life
never being truly alive

-koinophobia part 1-

living a half life
of breathing
and making money
without the adventures I had planned
and going to my deathbed
unsatisfied
wishing for a second chance
and finding no forgiveness there

-koinophobia part 2-

my fear of failing
of falling
stops me in my tracks
and keeps me
from getting anywhere
at all
I would rather
be nothing
than be wrong

-perfectionism ≠ productivity-

it's not that I don't trust you
it's that I don't trust myself
not to drive you away

it is so hard
to stop taking
and actually give

it is so hard
to let resentment go
and begin to forgive.

it is so hard
to see people for who they are
and not for what they did

-why is it so hard to be a good person?-

I learned to disconnect
at such a young age
that I'm not even sure anymore
what feelings are mine
and what has been taught to me

-the words "you're fine" were shoved down my
throat-

the universe shifts
things change
people grow
but I just roll over
in the grave I dug for myself

dear me in 10 years,

how are you? are you happy? do you make
enough money to pay the rent? do you still
talk to your friends? are you still writing? and
reading? and eating? did you ever go to Paris like
you said? drink coffee and eat too much bread?
when was the last time you talked to mom and
dad? do you miss home? do you laugh a lot? are
you taking your vitamins? are you still there?

-the letter I'm afraid to send-

sometimes the night is too long
and you have to look up at the stars
and pretend they're the sun
so you can make it through

the stars

it's cold and the night sky is clear
I think of all that brought me here
I came out the other side of my dark
and now I'm ready to embrace my stars

too many nights were spent
begging for an end
when all I really wanted
was a new beginning

-no more-

today marks
a new age
a new game
ready to play
I've survived
what they've thrown at me
settling in
is not my cup of tea

-change-

maybe it sounds superficial
fake
a fantasy
but I can feel the universe shifting
changing
making room for me

the hard times
will pass
and the light
will shine again
it is not the end
but the time to begin

on days when I don't know
how to love myself
they show me how

-*friends*-

I would drown myself
in written words
if not for them
they always keep me
from the deep end
and drag me back to life

we're reckless moons
stumbling in the sky
like butterflies from their cocoons
trying to find our why
we fall together
and fall apart
our souls untethered
we make reckless art

-teenagers-

I finally found friends
who love me for me
not for who I was
or who I could be
I finally found a reason
to make it through the night
because they showed me
what it's like to live in the light

thanks for helping me
begin to feel okay
it's so hard for flowers to grow
in such a dark space
my petals are all wilted
but you're helping me through the days
which now shine bright
with your beautiful sunrays

one day you're going to be driving home from
your best friends house listening to the radio
and it's going to hit you how far you've come and
you're going to realize that you stayed alive for this
and you're going to think *I made it here I made it
here I made it—*

we dance like flowers
in the rain
we relish the power
but they think we're just insane
we waltz with thunder
and mingle with lightning
our laughs spark with wonder
we feel our souls brightening
we spin with the raindrops
this is how we feel alive
we feel like we're on top
how could we ever think we wanted to die?
when there's storms like this
and 2am conversations
and love's first kiss
why can't we break free of our desperation?
desperation to live
desperation to thrive
when we just need to forgive
and not deny
that we were there

and now we're here
but we can go anywhere
if not we fear

home is waking up to the rain
and drifting right back down
home is laughing over coffee
and old places newly found
it's standing around a bonfire
and singing off-key
it's the late night conversations
shared between you and me
it's finally finishing that book
late at night
and telling you all about it
and you're not bothered in the slight
it's rolling down hills with friends
and warm golden spring light
it's honeysuckle breezes
and writing poems at midnight
it's your smile
it's your laugh
it's having real friends
that stand up on your behalf
home is an inside joke

with all the girls
home is feeling like
you're someone's whole world
home is feeling loved
and feeling whole
it's feeling sunshine bloom
in your soul
because home is not a place
somewhere for your body to lay
home is a feeling
a feeling like you're worth the time of day

I'm still learning and growing
and the only thing I really know
is that I don't understand anything
but at least I have them
and that's everything

in a year
of uncertainty
and fear
the only thing
I really know
is you're always here

when the world gets to be
too busy
or too much
I burrow into my father's jacket
several sizes too big
and inhale his cologne
and I think of his hugs
of his words
and keep going

-I hope you don't mind me stealing your jackets-

just because
they've been there your entire life
does not mean
they deserve to be there for the rest

*-something I learned from a toxic friendship, a
friend in an unhappy relationship, and an abused
child-*

now is the best place
you can be
climb to the top
and see all there is to see
be present
be here
feel the love
and the fear
stop thinking
and just feel
because you'll never get this view again
and nothing will ever be more real

what's the meaning of life?
how should I know?
I've only lived 16 years worth
but here's what I do know:

find your soulmates
I don't mean a boyfriend or girlfriend
friends
friends who are so naturally themselves
and so kind and welcoming
that you begin to feel comfortable with being yourself too
that you begin to trust in good people again

some will come and go
they are not soulmates
rather, they're subplots in your story
meant to teach you something

true soulmates
will see you in all your stages of growth

the rooting and sprouting and blooming
and, yes, even the wilting, right before you start new
and never love you less

find them
keep them
learn from them
teach them
this is the most important thing I know

-find your soulmates-

take a deep breath
and empty your plate
of all that you have to do

take a deep breath
and empty your plate
and find time to focus on you

don't cut your own legs out from under you
just to give them stilts
don't tear up your roots
just to stand in their shadow
don't empty yourself
so they can be full

-sometimes it's okay to be selfish-

don't trim yourself
to fit a pot
that you outgrew

-expand-

hang on just a little longer
happiness is on its way
because if we can count on the dark of night
we can count on the light of day

-full circle-

used to

when you asked me

what I wanted to do for a living

my answer was

I don't

I don't want this living

I don't want these air filled lungs

and this beating heart

now if you ask me

I tell you I want to write

I tell you I want to paint

I tell you I want to travel

I tell you I want to hold this world's attention

even for just a second

you ask me

what do you want to do for a living?

and I say

I want to live

the stars and moon take me back to the core of
humanity

I will stop depending
on other people for happiness
because I'm the only one
who hears what I hear
sees what I see
and feels what I feel at midnight
when my mind is too tired to filter itself
and I let my guard down
I am the only one
who can build that bridge
heal that wound
I'm the only one who can truly
fully make myself happy
I can't rely on family or friends
books or social media
or anything or anyone
because they don't hear
the ugly things I say about myself
when midnight strikes
and my mind is too tired to filter itself

take whiteout to the page
from dear mom to dear me
from tears and rage
to hopefully
I took my goodbye
and made it hello
and as the world sighed
I rewrote the bones

-suicide note-

I sit on the rooftop
above everything I know
and below everything I don't
I look into the eyes of the man in the moon
I whispered to him my story
the stars were leaning in pretty soon
I told them about the times I cried
and when I wished I had died
I told them about the times I laughed
and what it was at
I told them about my friends
who I would love to the very end
I told them why I was here
on a night so clear
because sometimes we don't need a hero
who goes out in a blaze of glory

-sometimes we just need a survivor story-

I write

otherwise

I would never say a thing

I am a quiet and opinionated creature

I used to think
I could cut the sadness out of me
or starve it to death
but now I laugh it out
and it falls off my shaking shoulders
now I paint it out
and it turns lifeless on the canvas
now I write it out
and it becomes powerless under my pen

I'm finding a new beat
playing a new song
getting to know me
and learning to dance along

-self love is my new favorite song-

it's weird
how life happens
how time can move so fast
it feels like a carpet snatched from underneath us
it's hard to catch your breath
in a world that never stops
things can feel so permanent
but then they're gone
it can feel like the end of the world
but then it's not
the world doesn't stop
even when it feels like yours is ending
burning
and over
and that can be a good thing
being forced to move on
the day ends
the world keeps on spinning
and it all comes around again
things that feel so impossible
and so far away

are suddenly so close
because the world the clock the cycle the wheel
doesn't stop
it doesn't pause
it forces you to move forward
and
even if you're not ready for it
tomorrow always comes

I no longer have to hide in the pages of a book
to hide from my thoughts and myself
I wake up smiling at the sun everyday
getting ready to start over
just because I know I can

I wake before the Sun
and meet him at the door
it's the start of a new beginning
I can feel it in my core
cup of coffee and a deep breath
this is what I've been waiting for

do you ever just feel lost
in a crowd?
like your head will never get out
of the clouds?
like your entire world is crumbling
down?
and then you have a realization
so profound
that your fate is not set, your soul
is not bound
that who you truly are
is yet to be found

-you are not set in stone-

do you ever just
get the sudden urge
to rip your soul from your body
and scrub it clean
so that it's all fresh
and good as new
so that you can start over
as someone else?

I remember one time
you had apologized
for the time we were strangers
and I was uncomfortable around you
and I had said
"it's okay
because flowers can't grow without rain"
you told me I had a beautiful mind
months later
I forgot the advice
I had given myself
I forgot that
you were just another rainy day
and once you were gone
I began to grow

note to self

Don't compare. You've never seen them at their worst.

I think there's some part of me still missing
and I think that's okay
maybe life is spent trying to find your missing piece
maybe life is being okay with never being complete
and learning to love yourself unfinished

I'm learning
to dance in my dark
meaning
I'm learning
to dance towards my light
enjoying every step of the way
even though I'm blind

I am here
and that is something
and I thank Him for that
every single day

love yourself
before you love anyone else
know your worth
before you let someone else
decide it for you

note to self

Respect yourself more than you resent them.

note to self

What they think doesn't define what I'm worth.

I can wish I'd never met you
but it's not really true
I needed the heartache
to test if I would break

-I didn't-

she wouldn't recognize me
if me from 3 years ago
or 2 years ago
or even a few months ago
could see me now
she wouldn't recognize me
she wouldn't see
the determination in my eyes
in her own
and she wouldn't look
at my smiling face
and think it hers
she has no idea
how far she's come
and how far she has to go

note to self

Speak your truth, even if you don't believe it yet.

little things
are what kept me going
my morning cup of coffee
rereading my favorite book
my best friend's laugh
watching my favorite show
no reason
is too small
to stay alive for
just keep going
because they're worth it
and so are you

reasons I'm glad I'm still alive

- I've laughed at a lot of jokes
- I've read a lot of good books
- I've heard a lot of good songs
- I've made a lot of new, wonderful friends
- I got to fall in love
- I got to fall out of love
- I got to fall in love with life instead
- I've drank a lot of good coffee
- I've laughed so hard my stomach hurt
- I've seen so many pretty sunrises and sunsets
- I get to see the stars and the moon
- I've read some beautiful poems
- I've gotten to see my friends grow and laugh and live
- I've started to learn to love myself
- I'm learning that I can be loved

note to self

I am flawed. I am human. I am beautiful. They are one in the same.

I lay awake at night and dream of her
the same yet we differ
stronger and smarter
yet I am a part of her
the way a crater is a part of the moon
she couldn't come too soon
then I'll just be a story
maybe she'll adore me
maybe she'll tuck away my photos and letters
maybe it'll be for the better
I'll melt away completely
they'll think they've defeated me
till she emerges anew
where's the girl that we knew
that weak little light
near the end of her life
we tell her she's not good enough
but we never saw how tough
she'd become
she let us think we won
and then the dying star

who travelled long and far
shriveled and burst
into her new universe
she reinvents
it is what's meant
to be
because I am her and she is me

-reborn-

you have to love your winter
as much as your spring and fall
sometimes you have to love your winter
most of all

I wished so hard
for a prince
who would save me
sweep me off my feet
I forgot that I myself
am the dragon
as well as the princess
I asked him to slay
the strongest part
of myself
for fear that my fire
would keep him away

dear younger me
I just want you to know
that one day you will be happy
and that your smile won't be for show

dear younger me
I just wanted to tell you
one day your laugh will be carefree
and you'll find friends who love you too

dear younger me
I hope you are well
you have so much more to see
and I have so much more to tell

my head is in the clouds
and it's not coming down
because down there it's too loud
and they strip me of my crown

so I'll watch from above
and breathe in the sunrays
and I'll fall in love
with all my cloudy days

I read my old notebooks and journals and I caressed the tear stained pages and I kissed the smudged words the way I wished I could hug and kiss younger me. I held her soul in my hands much gentler than any one in her life had, and I added notes on every page, telling her that things got better and telling her that she was worth it and that her life was worth it, as if she would be able to hear me, all those years ago.

I wish I could tell you
about all the good things to come
I wish you could see
where we are now
how far we've come
the friends we have
the nights spent singing
coffee in cafes at 10pm
hours laughing
and expressing
and thinking
I'm glad I stuck around for this
I want you to see the light
at the end of the tunnel
which seems infinite
I want you to know
that one day
you will be who you wished to be
for so long
and you will be
where you always wanted to be

I wish I could tell you
but you'll find out soon

-love, future you-

I've so often
mistaken
the end of a chapter
for the end of the world

I have days
where I feel insane
where my mind and body
ache with pain
but I keep going
and I won't complain
because things can't grow
without a little rain

after years
of emptiness
of coldness
of loneliness
I made myself at home
filled the place with flowers
started a fire in the hearth
and got to know myself again

why did it take me
so long to realize that
I deserve the stars

I kept feeling
like the book was not finished
that it would never be finished
but I was trying to force an end
on an unfinished journey
I don't know where I'm going
or how to get there
but at least I'm not where I was
and that's enough
for me
for now
because I am growing
and I am healing
and I am whole
and I am not done

-to be continued-

Aaliyah Vines is the author of *You Deserve The Stars*. Aaliyah lives in Louisiana, where she attends Haynesville High. She can often be found drinking coffee and stressing about her schoolwork. She can also be found on her instagram, tumblr, and her blog, where she posts book reviews, writing and life updates, and her thoughts on mental health and self-love. Aaliyah is happiest when reading, writing, and talking about the universe with her closest friends.